Ruby's Birds

For Anya, Niko, Ruby, and all of our planet's young caretakers who are ready to make some noise.

—M.T.

For Michael, Yolanda, and Arthur who fill me with inspiration, joy, and wonder.

—C.D.

Designed by Patricia Mitter
Edited by Jill Leichter

Hard Cover ISBN: 978-1-943645-33-6; Paperback ISBN: 978-1-943645-62-6

Printed in the United States of America

10 9 8 7 6 5 4

TheCornellLab Publishing Group

Produced by the
Cornell Lab Publishing Group
321 Glen Echo Lane, Ste. C
Cary, NC 27518

www.CornellLabPG.com

WunderMill

The Cornell Lab Publishing Group
is an imprint of WunderMill, Inc.
WunderMillBooks.com

CPSIA tracking label information
Production Location: CG Book Printers
North Mankato, Minnesota
Production Date: XXXXXX
Cohort: Batch No. 294313

By buying products with the FSC label you are supporting the growth of responsible forest management worldwide.

Ruby's Birds

By Mya Thompson

Illustrated by Claudia Dávila

TheCornellLab Publishing Group

School's out.
Mom and Dad are at work.
My brother, Malik, is at soccer practice.
Grandma's at her spot near the window.
Alex keeps her company.
Things are too quiet around here...

I know what to do.

I play the piano,
the piece my parents say is very grown up.

I practice my dance routine,
the one Malik calls stomping.

I talk with Alex,
in the secret language Grandma taught us.

I sing at the top of my lungs,
the song I made up myself.

My neighbor Eva from downstairs
hears everything.
She calls up from her window,
"Ruby! Wanna go to the park?"

"Yes, yes, yes, yes, yessss!"
I sing.

We pass my favorite bakery.

We pass CeCe's apartment.

We walk right past my regular park,
the one with the twisty slide and the sprinklers.
I guess Eva is going to a different park.
I skip to keep up.

I follow her all the way to Central Park,
where my parents sometimes take us
on Sundays when we're all dressed up.

Eva is going to the woods.
I've never been that way.

We sing made-up songs about joggers,
and strollers, and fancy dogs.

Bee, buzz, buzz, buzz

Suddenly, Eva stops.
She looks up.
She is listening.

I quiet down and I listen too.
What's wrong? I wonder.
I hear a police car, a plane, some barking.

I tug on Eva's sleeve, but she's not paying attention.
She holds her binoculars up to her eyes.
She is frozen like a statue.

And then, she smiles a huge smile.

I guess everything's okay, so I start singing again.

"Ruby!" Eva sighs, "You scared him away!"

"Who did I scare away?" I ask.

Eva flops down on a bench. I sit too.
"It's a bird I've only ever seen back home in Costa Rica," she says.
"He's just stopping through on his way north because this is the best patch of woods for miles around. He's quite a singer, just like you."

"If you stay quiet, we may be able to find him again.
He's a Golden-winged Warbler."

I nod.
I don't say a word. Or sing a word either.
It sounds like something from a fairy tale.

We move carefully. We're serious. We pay attention.

We watch for tiny movements in the leaves. We try and try.

"No luck today," says Eva, "but now you know what to do."

I sing myself to sleep as usual.

On Sunday morning,
I beg for a walk to Central Park.
Malik's not interested.
But it's family time, so he has to come anyway.

We pass the bodega.
We pass the theater.
I sing my song. My family listens along.

At the park, I lead them straight to the woods.
I'm silent. I'm serious. I'm paying attention.

I hear a rustle in the leaves.

"Shhhhhhh!" I say.

Just like Eva, I'm frozen like a statue.

A tiny bird pops out of the leaves.
It looks one way, then the other, then right at me.

I can't help it.
I get that huge smile just like Eva's.

"LOOK!" I yell.
"Ah, yes!" says Grandma.

"I saw a warblerrrr!" I sing, as he flies away.

ABOUT THIS STORY

As a brand-new bird watcher, Ruby is lucky to live near Central Park, one of the best places in the world to enjoy birds. You can find more than 280 kinds of birds there, if you know where to look and how to listen! It's mind-boggling to think that so many bird species live right in the center of New York City, one of the busiest cities in the world.

Some birds, like robins, starlings, and crows, stick around all year. Others, like the warblers, use the park mostly as a stopover in spring to rest and eat before they continue their migration north to nest and raise their own family.

Warblers are a group of small songbirds famous for their high-pitched "warbling." Eva has a feeling that Ruby will love getting to know a bird that likes to sing as much as she does.

When Eva hears the *Bee-buzz-buzz* song of a male Golden-winged Warbler in Central Park's North Woods, it reminds her of the comforting forest sounds back home in Costa Rica, where this bird spends the winter. She grew up calling warblers *reinitas* or "little queens," and gets a burst of joy every time she finds one. She also knows that these warblers are becoming rarer and rarer in the wild, so she is grateful to see that this one has safely made its journey from Central America.

LEARN MORE | *AllAboutBirds.org* | *CentralParkNYC.org*

Ruby's Birds

ABOUT BIRDS AT HOME

Ruby's pet, Alex, is a Sulphur-crested Cockatoo—an intelligent, social, and long-lived species native to Australia. In Ruby's house, Alex is part of the family, and gets to spend lots of time out of his cage.

As pets, cockatoos can learn all sorts of words, like the greeting "Wa gine on?" that Ruby's grandma from Barbados taught Alex. Because cockatoos become very attached to people who care for them and can live as long as humans, having one as a pet is a BIG responsibility.

Luckily, Sulphur-crested Cockatoos are not endangered, but sadly, other parrot species are becoming rare in the wild because so many people want them as pets. Before getting a pet bird, make sure it comes from a licensed captive breeder.

FIND BIRDS IN YOUR CITY

You can find lots of birds in your city if you know where to look and listen, and there are many common city birds hiding in the pages of this book. Ruby hasn't noticed them yet, but you will, once you look closely!

The birds you'll find are all favorites of the **Celebrate Urban Birds** project, a citizen-science project hosted by the Cornell Lab of Ornithology. Celebrate Urban Birds connects people to birds and the natural world through neighborhood activities and the arts.

You can celebrate birds near you by finding these species at your local park, playground, or near your favorite sidewalk tree. Be sure to share your discoveries with us by following the easy instructions on the project's website: *CelebrateUrbanBirds.org*

FIND THESE BIRDS IN THIS BOOK—AND IN YOUR CITY!

Just act like Eva and Ruby. You'll find them.

1
BROWN-HEADED COWBIRD
Find cowbirds at your local park perched up high, or in a flock on the ground pecking the grass for seeds and insects.

2
BLACK-CROWNED NIGHT-HERON
Go straight to a creek or pond near you, then look along the edge of the water to find a night-heron ready to snag a fish.

3
MALLARD
Head to a pond or lake and you'll find these ducks skimming their beaks along the surface, collecting insects and water plants.

4
AMERICAN CROW
You can find crows pretty much anywhere. That's because they'll eat pretty much anything. Just look up—and listen for their *caw-caw* calls.

5
PEREGRINE FALCON
Scan the rooftops and other high perches for these birds of prey. They watch from above and dive down to snatch smaller birds in mid-air.

6
BALTIMORE ORIOLE
Your best bet for finding these songbirds is a trip to the local park. They like to build their sock-shaped nests in the upper branches of trees.

7
MOURNING DOVE
Look down to find these doves eating seeds and crumbs they find on the ground. Listen for their *hooeeoo, hoo, hoo, hoo* calls.

8
ROCK PIGEON
Pigeons are easy to see in the city. You'll find them on sidewalks searching for bits of leftover food and sheltering together on building ledges.

9
HOUSE FINCH
If you put up a bird feeder, chances are you'll attract these finches. Watch for them perching in trees nearby, waiting for their chance to dine.

10
EUROPEAN STARLING
Sit on a bench and watch for starlings on a branch waiting for someone to drop some crumbs, or zig-zagging across the grass looking for insects.

11
AMERICAN ROBIN
In spring, you'll see robins plucking worms from grassy lawns. In winter, spot them in fruiting trees and bushes in your local park.

12
CEDAR WAXWING
Go to the park when the berries are ripe—the waxwings love them. They move in groups, so when you've found one, you'll probably find more.

13
HOUSE SPARROW
Watch the sidewalk for a hop-hop-hop near some leftover food. City sparrows are so used to people, you may even see one land on your windowsill.

14
GOLDEN-WINGED WARBLER
Visit city parks often in early spring, when all kinds of warblers stop to rest and fatten up before traveling north to nest in wilder places.

RUBY'S TIPS
for taking a nature walk

1 Get your family excited to go outside for a nature walk any way you know how. Chances are, they'll be happy to hear that you want some fresh air and family time.

If they say, "But there's not much to look at around here," remind them that there are animals and plants everywhere, and you don't have to travel outside your city or town to go on a nature walk.

If they say, "But we don't have time today," ask them when they will have time, then put it on the calendar.

2 On your walk, find a place to rest, then stay still and listen for a few minutes. Challenge everyone to count how many different sounds you hear—including birds, dogs, cars, even airplanes—all of it!

3 Or try a *rainbow walk*—that's where you look for things in nature that match the colors you can see in a rainbow.

4 Take pictures and make recordings of what you see and hear as you go (that way, you can look things up later). You can even make sketches of what you see.

Remember!

Don't let your adults get discouraged if they don't know what kinds of plants, insects, mushrooms, or birds you see and hear. Offer a hug and remind them that it's all about having fun and noticing new things.

The**Cornell**Lab of Ornithology